Judy Moody
Goes to College

Judy Moody

Goes to College

Megan McDonald

illustrated by
Peter H. Reynolds

CANDLEWICK PRESS

Text copyright © 2008 by Megan McDonald
Illustrations copyright © 2008 by Peter H. Reynolds
Judy Moody font copyright © 2003 by Peter H. Reynolds

Judy Moody®. Judy Moody is a registered trademark of Candlewick Press, Inc.

First paperback edition in this format 2018

Library of Congress Cataloging-in-Publication Data is available.
Library of Congress Catalog Card Number 2007052207

ISBN 978-0-7636-4856-5 (hardcover)
ISBN 978-1-5362-0078-2 (paperback)

21 22 23 24 25 TRC 10 9 8 7 6 5

Printed in Eagan, MN, U.S.A.

This book was typeset in Stone Informal and Judy Moody.
The illustrations were done in watercolor, tea, and ink.

Candlewick Press
99 Dover Street
Somerville, Massachusetts 02144

visit us at www.candlewick.com

For Sophia and Emily
M. M.

Dedicated to Beatrice Rose Scollan,
Desmond Patrick Scollan, and
Beth "Ginger Betty" Veneto, who
deserve honorary degrees for
their community service!
P. H. R.

Table of Contents

Who's

Judy Moody

Tutor tot.
Rare to the tenth power.

Dad

aka Richard.
Old skool.

Mom

aka Kate.
One-half of the 'rents.

Mouse

Yoga (not yogurt) Cat

Who

Stink
The original geck = annoying person.

Frank

The peeps.

Rocky

Chloe
Sick-awesome college student. Judy's *uber*-rare tutor.

Math-i-tude

When Judy Moody got to school on Monday, she had a new teacher. Her new teacher was called a sub (not the sandwich). Her new teacher was called Mrs. Grossman. Exactly three things were wrong with that. (1) Mrs. *Gross*man was NOT gross. (2) Mrs. Gross*man* was NOT a man. (3) Mrs. Grossman was NOT Mr. Todd.

Judy was the first to raise her hand. "Where's Mr. Todd?"

"I'm sure Mr. Todd told everyone on Friday that he was going to a special teacher conference."

"I wasn't here Friday," said Judy.

"He's going to learn to be a better teacher," said Jessica Finch.

"But Mr. Todd's already a great teacher," said Judy.

"Maybe he's getting a special teacher award," said Rocky.

"Where did he go?" Judy asked. "And when will he be back?"

The others joined in. "Are you going to read us *Catwings*? Mr. Todd always reads us *Catwings*. And *Catwings Return*."

"Are you going to take us on field trips? Mr. Todd always takes us on field trips."

"Are we still Class 3T? Or are we Class 3G now?"

"Mr. Todd is in Bologna, Italy," said Mrs. Grossman.

Sheesh. Life was no fair. Judy liked baloney (the sandwich). Judy liked Italy. She even knew a special dance from Italy— the tarantella. Mr. Todd was probably in the Land of Baloney right now, dancing like a tarantula, while they were stuck in the Land of Multiplication, learning boring old times tables.

She, Judy Moody, did not like third grade, Class 3T-that-was-now-3G, without Mr. Todd.

Judy Moody's new teacher came from

4

New England. She did not talk like Mr. Todd. She talked funny, with a lot of extra *r*'s. Judy Moody's new teacher did not wear cool glasses like Mr. Todd. She wore glasses hanging from a chain around her neck. She did not even smell like Mr. Todd. She smelled like she took a bath in P.U. perfume.

Judy Moody's new teacher put up a tent in the back of the room with a sign that said ATTITUDE TENT. Judy wondered what attitude they had to be in to get to go camping.

And . . . Judy Moody's new teacher was cuckoo for candy. She gave out candy for good behavior to everybody (minus Judy,

because she was in a mood). She even gave out candy for the right answers in math. Pretty soon, the whole class was going to have math cavities. Except for Judy.

Today, Mrs. Grossman was talking about measure. Quarts and gallons and barrels and hogsheads. She tried to make it sound like math was a barrel of fun. But Judy, for one, did not give a pig's ear about hogsheads.

Mrs. Grossman wore ten gallons of perfume.

Mrs. Grossman gave out twenty hogsheads of candy.

Instead of listening, Judy played with her watch. Her brand-new, fancy-dancy, robin's-egg-blue, glow-in-the-dark Ask-a-Question

Watch 5000, complete with predict-the-future answers and screen saver.

Blah, blah, blah, said Mrs. Grossman. Rounding numbers up, rounding numbers down. Judy *estimated* that *rounding* did not make math one bit easier.

Judy pressed some buttons. A night-light blinked. A dual-time button gave the time in TWO countries so a person did not have to wear two different watches.

Scribble, scribble. Mrs. Grossman scratched on the board for a math-ternity.

Judy pressed the big green question-mark button.

Rare! It was just like the Magic 8 Ball. Ask the watch a question, press the glow-in-the-dark green button, and it gave you mystery answers.

Is Mrs. Grossman cuckoo for math?

YOU BET.

Is Mrs. Grossman ever going to give me candy?

CAN'T TELL.

Am I going to college someday?

LOOKS GOOD.

Is Mr. Todd ever coming back?

HAZY.

"Judy? Did you hear the question?"

Judy did not hear the question. So Judy did not know the answer.

Was it 77? 88? 99? Gallons? Bathtubs? Barrels? Pigs' heads?

Judy blurted the only answer that sprang to mind.

"Hazy!" she called out.

Mom- and Dad-i-tude

She, Judy Moody, had to take a note home. A note from the teacher. A note that said she needed extra-special help. A note that said she was hazy-not-crazy about math.

The top half of the note was just *blah-blah,* so Judy tore the note in half and gave the good half to her parents. Not the bad half. Mom and Dad looked at the note.

"Judy's in trouble? Sweet!" said Stink.

"Only *half* trouble," said Judy.

"Judy, where's the rest of this note?" asked Dad.

"I rounded it down," said Judy. "To one-half. Like the fraction. Get it? I'm really good at math. Fractions and rounding and everything."

"Quick! What's twelve times eight?" asked Stink.

"None of your beeswax," said Judy.

"Try ninety-six," said Stink.

"Judy, the note?" Mom said. "Dad and I need to see it. The *whole* thing."

Judy reached into her pocket and pulled out the crumpled-up bottom half of the note. She handed it over.

Mom and Dad read it. They read it times two. It took them about one thousand years to read the fraction of a note.

They talked to Judy. They talked to each other. They talked to people on the phone for a hundred years. They came up with a plan.

Not a Listen-to-Your-New-Teacher plan.

Not a Hand-Over-Your-Brand-New-Watch plan.

Not a We'll-Help-You-with-Your-Homework plan.

An Extra-Extra-Special Help plan. *EESH!* A Judy-Moody-Goes-to-a-Tutor plan.

"Tutor?" said Judy. "Can't you and Dad help me?"

"We will," said Mom.

"We will," said Dad.

"What's six times seven?" said Stink.

"A tutor will be extra help," said Mom.

"A tutor will be special help," said Dad. "Just like your teacher suggested."

"For your information," said Judy, "Mrs. Grossman is NOT my teacher."

"What's five times eleven?" asked Stink.

"I'll listen, I promise," said Judy. "I won't wear my new watch to school anymore. I'll count to gross and great gross."

"*You're* gross," said Stink.

Judy had to prove she was good at math. She started rattling off times tables.

"Four times two equals eight. Eight times two equals sixteen. Sixteen times two equals something I haven't learned yet. But I will. I swear."

"Having a tutor could be fun," said Dad. "You'll see."

"*Tutors* have *flash cards*," said Stink. "*Baby* flash cards. What's two times five?"

"The number of toenails I'm going to paint while you're asleep," said Judy. Stink curled his toes under.

Judy looked from Mom to Dad, from Dad to Mom. "Do I have to?"

"It's already settled," said Mom. "You start tomorrow."

"Hogsheads!" said Judy.

❧   ❧   ❧

Dad picked up Judy after school the next day. Judy closed her eyes and slumped in the backseat of the car on the way to the tutor's. All she could see behind her closed eyes were flash cards. *Baby* flash cards. She, Judy Moody, was in a mood. Not a math mood. And definitely NOT a flash card mood.

Fact of Life: She, Judy Moody, was a Tutor Tot.

"Am I going to have to count beads and glue macaroni? Stink says I am going to have to count beads and glue macaroni."

16

"I don't know," said Dad.

"Am I going to have to play with jelly beans in jars? Stink says I'm going to have to play with jelly beans in jars," said Judy.

"I don't know," said Dad.

"Am I going to have to make a cat out of a triangle? Stink says I'm going to have to make a cat out of a triangle."

"Let's wait and see," said Dad. "Maybe you'll get to play math games—like tic-tac-toe."

Tic-tac-toe-nails! Judy made a mad face and slumped down in the seat some more. Dad didn't get it. He didn't have to spend his afternoon doing macaroni math and making geometry cats.

"We're here!" Dad called cheerfully.

"Where's here?" Judy asked in a moody tone.

"Colonial College," said Dad.

"College?" asked Judy.

"That's where you'll get help with your math," said Dad. "Your tutor is a college student."

Judy bolted upright and threw her arms in the air. "I'm going to college!"

Mad-i-tude

Judy followed Dad down the tree-lined sidewalks of the Colonial College campus, stepping on every crack she could find *on purpose.* They went past a duck pond with a fountain, a serious library with a clock tower, and a way-cool giant sculpture of bacon and eggs. Finally, they came to a four-story brick building with pointy towers that looked like a castle covered in ivy.

"This is it," said Dad. "Grace Brewster Murray Hopper Hall."

They wound their way upstairs and down long hallways to a door that said MATH LAB.

"Here we are!" said Dad.

A girl with green eyes and a messy ponytail greeted them. "You must be the Moodys."

"I'm Richard Moody, and this is my daughter, Judy," said Dad.

"Hi, I'm Chloe. Chloe Canfield. My friends call me C-squared, since my name has two Cs and I go to CC. You know, C to the second power, 'cause I'm into math?"

"That's funny," said Dad, shaking her hand.

"I don't get it," said Judy.

"It's algebra," Chloe said.

"Algebra? Didn't any-body tell you? I'm only in third grade."

Chloe laughed. "It just means when you multi-ply something by itself, you say it's squared, or to the second power."

"Oh, yeah. If I'm in a mood, like a double bad mood, then it's called a bad mood squared, right?"

"That's right. Moody to the second power," said Chloe. Dad bit his lip.

"Rounding off, squaring stuff, and big powers—yikes!" said Judy.

"That's what I'm here for," said Chloe. "Math is everywhere. Math is a fact of life. You'll see. It'll be fun."

"I don't know." Judy saw flash cards on the table. Where there were flash cards, triangle cats and macaroni could not be far behind.

"You'll be fine," said Dad, smoothing the top of Judy's hair. But Judy wasn't so sure. "I'll be back in an hour to pick you up."

"That's sixty whole minutes!" Judy cried.

"Yep. Three thousand six hundred seconds." Chloe led Judy over to an area where a table was piled with sponge blocks, color tiles, and (oh, no!) jars of counting bears and beads. For a split second, Judy had thought college was going to be cool. But this was *baby* college.

She, Judy Moody, was in a mood. Not a good mood. A bad mood squared. Moody to the power of ten million.

"This is Investigation Station," said Chloe.

Investigation Station was probably just another name for *Homework* Station.

"What looks good?" Chloe asked, pointing to shelves against the walls stuffed with games.

"You mean we get to play a game and I get to pick and we don't have to count jelly beans in a jar?"

"I knew if I made you paper—you know, fill out work sheets—you'd freak. I thought you'd be all over playing a game. Then we'd be crucial."

"Kru-shul?"

"You know. Good. Awesome."

"Oh, you mean *rare*. Let's play the Game of Life. It has a way-cool spinner."

"Rad," said Chloe. She stuck the box under her arm. "Let's go."

"Go where? Aren't we already there? On Investigation Station?"

"I know a better place to study math. It's called Coffee Catz."

Judy followed Chloe into the college coffee shop. Yum! It smelled like just-baked cookies and was packed with college kids reading, studying, and madly typing into laptops.

Chloe ordered a tall, skinny, nonfat, wet, extra-foam, no-whip latte with a double shot of vanilla (aka fancy-schmancy coffee drink), and Judy ordered a hot chocolate in a *bowl*. Chloe gave Judy a ten-dollar bill, and Judy got to pay like a grown-up and count the change. There was enough change to buy a candy cell phone at the counter.

At a window seat, Chloe spread out the board and Judy helped her snap in the mountains, bridges, and buildings. Chloe

gave Judy a car to drive (around the board, that is). "I love this game, because it's like life. You get to go to college and make money and buy a house."

"Rare," said Judy. "I already know I want to be a doctor."

"For serious?" Chloe asked. "In the game or in life?"

"Both," said Judy.

"So, you're premed. That's what they call it before you go to medical school. Or in your case, pre-premed."

"Premed squared," said Judy.

"One of my peeps wants to be a doctor," said Chloe.

"Peeps?"

"One of my friends. You know, if you're going to go to college, you're gonna have to learn to *talk* college."

"For serious?" Judy asked.

"*Zing!* You got me there," said Chloe, laughing.

In the Game of Life, Judy got to be the banker. "My little brother, Stink, ALWAYS gets to be banker," she told Chloe. She,

Judy-Moody-not-Stink, was in charge of piles and piles of money and got to dish out the big bucks. AND Chloe let her be a doctor, even though it was against the rules to peek at the Career cards.

Judy got to make a mountain of money and get married and buy a house and a high-def TV and learn sign language and find buried treasure and go to the Grand Canyon and help the homeless, and not once did a tree fall on her, not even a mid-life crisis.

"I love Life!" said Judy.

"You beat the pants off me," said Chloe.

"Speaking of pants," said Judy, "can I ask you a question? Why are you wearing a dress *and* pants?"

"It's my thing," said Chloe. "It's the artist in me."

"Is that why you wear flip-flops and have holes in your jeans and a flower tattoo and dyed-red hair and seven pierces?" Judy asked.

"Um, I guess so," said Chloe.

"Crucial!" said Judy.

❦   ❦   ❦

On the way back to the Math Lab, Chloe and Judy cut through the parking lot. "Look at all the VW Beetles!" said Judy. "One green, two reds, blue, yellow. My brother would go punch-buggy crazy!"

"So you like VW bugs?" Chloe asked. "Mine's the green one, right over there.

They call that color Gecko Green. I call her June Bug, because I got her last June."

"For serious? Sweet! It even has a real flower vase on the dashboard. Hey, did you know you're growing a toothbrush in your flower vase?" Judy cracked up.

"Tell you what," said Chloe. "Let's count all the Beetles in the parking lot and write down how many we can find of each color. Then we'll go back to the lab and I'll show you how to make a graph."

Judy raced around the parking lot, counting lots of red, blue, yellow, and green bugs. Only two silver Beetles and one gray. "The gray one looks like a robot!" said Judy.

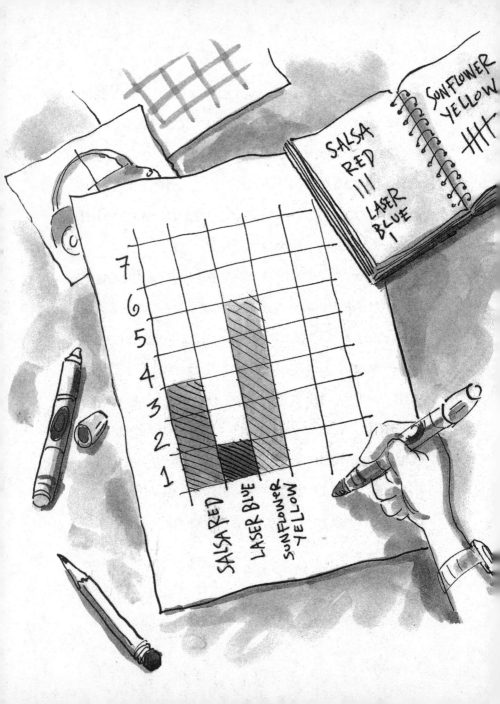

Back at the Math Lab, Judy made a graph and colored in squares for each kind of Beetle. Salsa Red, Laser Blue, Sunflower Yellow. . . . Judy forgot all about the time.

"Richard's here," said Chloe, nodding toward the door.

"Who's Richard?" Judy looked up and saw her dad standing in the doorway. "Is an hour up already?" she asked. "You were only gone for like a giga-flip-flop-second. Can't you stay away a little longer?"

"Having fun with math, huh?"

"I'm learning to make a graph, and when we're done, Chloe says I can hang it on the wall. It'll be graph-iti!"

A New Attitude

Judy could not wait to go back to college —
three times a week! Getting tutored was
crucial. Rare squared!

In just two short weeks, Judy had a
brand-new lease on life.

She, Judy Moody, sashayed into the
kitchen one morning before school. She
was wearing a dress on top of jeans ripped
at the knee, a teeny-tiny hoodie sweatshirt,

monkey flip-flops, a crazy scarf, skinny glasses, half a gross of bracelets, and tattoo Band-Aids.

"She must be in a play," said Stink.

"That's ridonkulus," said Judy. "Unless you mean the play of *life*."

"How many shirts are you wearing?" Stink asked.

"Is that my scarf?" Mom asked.

"I'm dressing for college," said Judy. "I have tutoring after school today, Kate." Chloe called grown-ups by their first names, so Judy tried it.

"It's too cold for flip-flops," Mom said, frowning.

"And you'll need a coat," Dad added.

Parents. Parental Units. The 'Rents. Kate

and Richard were so *old skool*. "College kids don't wear coats!" said Judy.

"What do they wear?" asked Stink.

"They wear whatever's their thing," said Judy.

"So your thing is to dress like a clown?" Stink asked.

Eesh! What an NCP. Nincompoop.

"How's it going with Chloe, by the way?" Mom asked.

"Chloe is the bomb! She drives a green gecko Beetle called June Bug and has fake red hair and a toe ring and seven pierces."

"Nobody needs that many extra holes in their head," said Dad.

"What a Swiss Cheese Head!" said Stink. "I already have seven holes in my head.

Two eyes plus two ears plus two nostrils plus one mouth equals seven."

"Does this Chloe know any math?" Mom asked.

"Does this Chloe have any flash cards?" asked Stink.

"For your information, we don't use flash cards," said Judy. "But we do play Multiplication Bingo and Tic-Tac-Cookie with Oreos. We even made a giant Sponge-Block Triangle Pants, and Chloe named him Turd Ferguson." Judy snorted. "It was so *money*."

"I don't see what a sponge named Turd Ferguson has to do with math," said Stink. "Right, Mom? Right, Dad?"

Fact of Life: Stink = annoying!

"Stink, it's sponge *blocks*. They were invented by a kid. See, you add up all the lines and angles, and it makes a polygon. You can use triangles, rectangles, and squares, too." Mom raised her eyebrows at Dad. Dad raised his eyebrows at Mom.

"Aw," said Stink. "Can I go to college, too?"

Judy ignored him. "Chloe says you can't be afraid of math," she told Kate and Richard. "You just have to practice, like piano, or soccer. *And* you can't give up. *And* you have to remember to have fun."

"Well, I like your attitude," said Mom.

"You mean my *math*-i-tude," said Judy, cracking herself up. "Chloe says math is everywhere. Math is life."

"Then you better get going," said Mom. "Don't want to be late for life."

⊚   ⊚   ⊚

On the way to school, Judy asked a question of her Ask-a-Question Watch 5000.

Will Mr. Todd be back today? She pressed the green button.

`DON'T KNOW.`

She tried again. *Will Mr. Todd be back today?*

`CAN'T TELL.`

She tried a third time. *Will Mr. Todd be back today?*

`NO WAY!`

When she got to school, she raced down the hall to her classroom. No Mr. Todd. No fair.

Mrs. Not-So-Great Grossman did not seem to appreciate Judy's new math-is-everywhere take on life. To make things even worse, she told the class that Mr. Todd broke his foot in Italy. (Probably from dancing the tarantella.) Mr. Todd would not be coming back for two more weeks.

As for the peeps, well, her friends were so UN-college. When they saw Judy's new outfit, they thought she was a scarecrow.

"What happened to your knees?" asked Rocky.

"Did you fall off your bike and rip your pants?" Frank asked.

"You must hurt bad—look at all those Band-Aids," said Amy Namey.

"Tattoos," Judy muttered.

"It's just a phase," said Rocky. "Like when she wore her pajamas to school."

"And her doctor coat," said Frank.

"And her pilgrim dress," said Jessica Finch.

"For your information," Judy pointed out, "kids in college wear pajama pants to class all the time. It's *rad*."

"It's red?" Rocky asked.

"It's rude?" Frank asked.

Sometimes third-graders were such *NCPs*.

"What stuff do you do with your tutor?" Amy asked.

"College stuff," said Judy. "We talk about algebra, and—"

"Algebra?!" said Jessica Finch. "Even I don't know algebra."

"It's no biggie. When I hang out with my college friend, I get to drink coffee and drive a car and talk on a cell phone."

"Whoa squared," said Amy Namey.

"Exactly," said Judy.

"You drink coffee?" asked Rocky.

"Actually, it's hot chocolate. But I do get to drink it at a coffee shop and order it and pay for it myself and count the change."

"Wow!" said Frank.

"No way did you drive a car," said Rocky.

"Yah-huh," said Judy. "No lie."

"You'd have to sit on like three phone books," said Frank.

"And get a license," said Jessica Finch.

"I got to drive a car in the Game of Life," said Judy.

"Oh," said Rocky. Amy and Jessica rolled their eyes.

"Judy does know how to drive," said Frank. "She's driving . . . us crazy!" Everybody cracked up.

Brat-i-tude

At morning recess, Judy faked a call on her candy cell phone. During Science, Judy drew a cartoon of Mrs. Grossman out of polygons.

At lunchtime, Judy said, "Let's food!" and waited in the lunch line with her peeps. When it was her turn, she stepped up to the window and said to the lunch lady, "I'll have a small-tall upside-down backward nonfat capp, extra whip. And make it wet."

"Aren't all drinks wet?" asked Frank.

"We don't have coffee," said the lunch lady.

"Hot chocolate?" Judy asked. But all they had was chocolate milk. *Bor-ing.* "At college, you can get hot chocolate with a heart design in the foam on top. And you can get sprinkles."

"Oh, really?" said the lunch lady.

"How many kinds of cereal do you have here?" Judy asked.

"None. We don't have any cereal. It's lunch."

"At college, you can have breakfast all

day. Even if it's midnight." Rocky, Frank, and Jessica pushed past Judy.

"Do you have a salad bar?" Judy asked.

"Salad bar is for teachers only."

"At college, anybody can eat at the salad bar. Even kids. What kind of cafeteria is this? They should call it cafe*terrible*."

"Hey, College," yelled a fifth-grader at the back of the line. "Move it along. Some of us want to eat lunch today."

Judy took her not-wet, no-whip, heartless chocolate milk and went to sit with her peeps.

"Shh, here she comes."

"What's she going to brag about now?"

"Yeah, she thinks she's so *college*."

Soon she, Judy Moody, was eating alone at the lunch table. Fact of Life: Rocky minus Frank minus Jessica Finch minus Amy Namey equaled a big fat zero. Not a *peep*.

Judy stared at her lunch tray. Her peanut butter and jelly sandwich looked so . . . kindergarten.

At recess, nobody wanted to play Judy's game — finding polygons

hidden on the playground. Judy found a triangle in a tree branch, an octagon where the fence was ripped, and six rectangles on the ladder going up to the slide.

All by herself.

For the first time ever, Judy could not wait for math class. She, Judy Moody, *owned* the times tables. *Look out. Here comes the Multiplication Maniac. The Polygon Princess. The Graph Guru. The Fraction Freak. Just wait till they see me score candy for all the right answers.*

At last it was time. Mrs. Grossman started writing on the board. Judy sat up straight. She pricked up her best-ever listening ears, the ones she usually saved for Mr. Todd. She squinted at the board.

Words? Why was Mrs. Grossman writing so many words? What did words have to do with math? *Hello?* Where were all the numbers?

And the fractions and the plus signs and the equal signs?

Judy raised her hand. "Excuse me," she said. "I thought this was math class. What's with all the sentences?"

"We're starting something new today," said Mrs. Grossman. "Multistep word problems. You have to read the problem first, then do the math one step at a time. That's why we call them *word* problems," said Mrs. Grossman.

Judy had a word problem, all right. A problem with words that were pretending to be math.

Mrs. Grossman pointed to the board. "Jill had twenty-four valentines. She gave one-half of her valentines to her friends at school—"

Judy raised her hand again. "Who's Jill?"

"Jill isn't a real person. She's just somebody in a word problem."

"So her name could be Chloe," said Judy. "And her school could be a college."

Mrs. Grossman shut her eyes and took a deep breath. "Judy, please let me finish. Then Jill gave the other half of her valentines to friends who live in her building, except for—"

Judy raised her hand again. "Building? Like maybe a dorm?"

"It doesn't matter. It's just an example."

"Will we get to draw a graph for this

word problem? With hearts for valentines?" asked Judy. "Because in college we get to draw graphs."

"Judy, I'm going to have to ask you again to stop interrupting."

"I was just saying . . ." said Judy.

Mrs. Grossman let out a big breath, but her face looked all pinched up. "Jill had enough valentines left over to give to her mom, her dad, and her little sister."

"Jill sounds like a pill," said Judy.

"Judy, that's it," said Mrs. Grossman. She pointed to the tent in the back of the room.

"You mean I have to go in that tent?"

"That's why we call it the Attitude Tent," said Mrs. Grossman.

"But I'm not really in a camping attitude," said Judy.

"Go sit in the tent. Don't come out until
you can show me an attitude adjustment.
And not another word about college,
Judy."

Eesh! Mrs. Grossman was the reason
she went to college in the first place. She
wished Mrs. Grossman would go back to
where she came from in the first place.
New England. Probably *Math*-a-chu-setts.

Judy hung her head and slunk to the
back of the room. She crawled inside the
tent. It was kind of like the Toad Pee Club
clubhouse inside. Minus any peeing toads,
of course. *Natch.*

She, Judy Moody, did not even play

with her Ask-a-Question Watch 5000. She thought about what she'd done, but she could not for the life of her understand why Mrs. G. didn't like her attitude. Didn't Mrs. Grossman know a positive math-i-tude when she saw one?

Now her math-i-tude had turned into a *mad*-i-tude.

Math was no fair. Math = life. Life was no fair.

See? A person could do multistep word problems even in an attitude tent. No biggie. You just had to have the right math-i-tude.

Not-So-Bad-i-tude

Judy Moody was down in the dumps. She had an attitude that was in the lower latitudes. A *bad-i-tude*.

"What's wrong?" Chloe asked her at tutoring that afternoon. "You hardly ate any of your pizza fractions."

"I have an attitude," said Judy.

"Everybody has an attitude," said Chloe. "It just means the way you think, the way you see things."

"The way I see things, Mrs. Grossman doesn't like my attitude. Mrs. Grossman says I need an attitude adjustment. So I went in the attitude tent, but all I got was a spider bite. All that did was adjust my attitude from bad to itchy."

"I know something that might help your attitude," said Chloe.

"Don't say algebra," said Judy.

"How would you like to come to college on Saturday?"

"Oh, no. You mean now I have to do math on the weekend, too?"

"Not for math, silly. I mean, how would you like to come spend the day with me at college? For fun."

Suddenly, she, Judy Moody, knew what an attitude adjustment felt like. It felt like when you went from a bad mood to a good mood. It felt like when your spider bite stopped itching. It felt like when you got to spend a whole, entire fun-not-math day at college.

Judy could not wait for Saturday.

֎   ֎   ֎

Judy woke up by mistake at six o'clock on Saturday morning, a not-school day. Chloe told her that college kids like to sleep late, so Judy tried to think like a college kid and go back to sleep. But it was no use.

"I don't see what the big-whoop deal is about college," said Stink. "All they do is carry heavy books around and listen to headphones. And if you go to college, you have to sleep over without Mom and Dad for like three or four years. And you have to wash your own clothes!"

For a kid who read the encyclopedia, Stink sure didn't know a lot. "Stink, you don't have the right *attitude* about college. Just wait till you're older and wiser, like me."

"When I'm older and wiser, will I eat cereal with a fork, too?"

"Oops," said Judy, opening the dish-washer to look for a spoon. By the time she got back to her bowl of cereal, her Mood Flakes had turned the milk pink.

Sweet! Pink milk (in Mood Flakes) was for *happy*. That was the first sign that she, Judy Moody, was about to have the time of her life.

Then Judy checked the Ask-a-Question Watch 5000 just to be sure.

Is today going to be the best day ever at college?

YUP!

She asked it again just to make sure and absolute positive.

NO DOUBT!

It was a sign, all right. A sign to the power of three.

❧   ❧   ❧

Judy followed Chloe up to her third-floor dorm room. The tiny room was chock-full of beds and desks and computers and books. Between bunk beds was an orange hairy rug, and on the beds were furry zebra-and-leopard-skin bedspreads. Posters covered the walls, even the ceiling.

There was a pink mini fridge and a mini TV and a mini microwave. Even a Bonjour Bunny alarm clock.

"Rare!" said Judy. "Your room is so orange and furry. Everything's cool-mini. You have bunk beds like me, only yours has a desk under it. And you have the Bonjour Bunny alarm clock radio night-light. Does it have a snooze button that lights up?"

A tall girl wearing pajama pants (same-same as Judy) came in and plopped down on a giant rubber-ball chair.

"Hey, roomie," Chloe said. "This is my

friend Judy Moody. Judy, this is my roommate, Bethany Wigmore."

Bethany Wigmore had long, dark hair
and large, dark eyes. Bethany Wigmore
wore headphones and lots of necklaces.
Bethany Wigmore had flip-flops with jewels on them!

"I like your flip-flops," Judy told her.

"Thanks. I made them."

"For serious?"

"It's easy," said Bethany Wigmore. "All
you need are fake jewels and beads and a
mini glue gun. C'mon, I'll show you."

Bethany Wigmore showed Judy Moody
how to make fancified flip-flops. Then she
said, "Now let's paint our toenails!"

"No, thanks," said Judy.

"We have *mood* nail polish," said Chloe. "It changes with your mood."

"I'm in!" said Judy. In no time, she, Judy Moody, had red-glitter toenails that turned purple. It was more impressive than sick, more powerful than rare. It was *sick-awesome*. *Mad-nasty!*

Who knew that having a roomie made life so way-not-boring?

"Let's food," said Chloe. "I'll take you to the dining hall, Judy. Then you can come to class with me."

"Class?" Judy asked. *Class* sounded semi-boring, even though *college class* sounded like something she could brag about later.

"Painting class," said Chloe. "It'll be fun. I promise."

Bethany Wigmore called after them, "Hit me up later!"

❧   ❧   ❧

On the way to lunch, they passed a big green patch of grass in the middle of the campus called the Quad. Every inch of it was filled with tents. Judy had never seen so many attitude tents. Was everybody in college in a bad mood?

"Did all the kids in these tents get in trouble and get sent to an attitude tent?" Judy asked.

"These aren't attitude tents," said Chloe. "This is a peace rally. Only instead of marching, people slept out in tents on the Quad last night to make a statement saying that they're for peace."

"I guess you could say they rested in peace," said Judy, grinning.

"Good one," said Chloe. "C'mon, let's go see my friend Paul."

There were drummers drumming and dancers dancing and people waving signs—all for peace. Chloe's friend Paul was one of the drummers. He let Judy make loads of noise on a bongo drum, and she got to Hula-Hoop for peace and even tie-dye a shirt. On the front she drew a peace sign and wrote PEACE IS CRUCIAL.

They waited for Judy's shirt to dry, but Chloe finally said, "This is as much fun as

watching paint dry, huh? Let's check out the yoga tent."

The yoga tent had a very peace-full attitude. Judy learned to make shapes with her arms and legs. She got to pretend to be a cat, a mountain, a chair, and a not-math triangle.

"Who knew peace could be so much fun?" said Judy, wriggling into her PEACE IS CRUCIAL shirt over her I ATE A SHARK shirt.

Next stop: cafeteria. Judy ate one pancake with three colors of syrup, a salad from the NOT-teachers-only salad bar, and half of Chloe's burger, which was made of vegetables (minus eggplant). No lie!

She did not have to wait in line, she did not have to get bossed by bossy fifth-graders, and she did not have to eat boring old PBJ sandwiches that were so *kindergarten,* like at the cafe*terrible.* Who knew that veggies (smushed up on a bun with ketchup) could taste so *rad?*

Art-i-tude

"Oops, we better not be late for class," said Chloe. They raced across campus to the art building. Judy followed Chloe down a long hall lined with colorful lockers. They passed a pottery class where people were spinning clay on wheels, a sculpture class where students were making buildings out of bubble wrap, and a . . . naked lady class!

Judy squeezed her eyes shut. "Please tell me we are NOT going to Naked Lady Class."

Chloe almost spit out her coffee. "It's Life Drawing. To be an artist, you have to learn to draw real life."

"When I draw Real Life, it is NOT going to be bare-naked," said Judy.

In painting class, Judy got to sit next to Chloe in a dark room and watch a slide show of paintings. There were paintings of bones and giant sunflowers and swirly-twirly night skies. Even soup cans. There were paintings of cut-paper leaves and moons and paintings that looked like spilled cans of paint, even though the teacher (that everybody had to call professor) said it was a masterpiece. There were black-and-white paintings of birds that hurt your eyes if you stared at them too much.

"These paintings are psycho!" Judy said, cracking herself up. Chloe put her finger to her lips.

"In third grade, you're not allowed to talk when the teacher is talking either," Judy whispered. "Same-same!"

The teacher, Mr. Professor-Who-Likes-Psycho-Paintings, was yakking on forever about shadows in every picture. Shadows this and shadows that. Shadows here and shadows there. Shadows seemed to be very-way-important in art.

When the slide show and the yakking

were over, everybody got to make paintings of their own. (Finally!)

Judy got to stand next to Chloe at a tall
table and make a big giant mess. At college, it did not matter if paper scraps got all
over the table. At college, it did not matter
if paint dripped all over the floor. And at
college, it did not matter how many sup-
plies you used, even a whole entire bottle
of sparkly-blue glitter glue.

Chloe said worrying about rules was *old
skool.* Chloe said art is life and life is messy,
so art should be messy.

At college, all that mattered was that
you (1) use your imagination (which Judy
had loads and loads of) and (2) be yourself.
Who else would she, Judy Moody, be?

Judy was so busy using her imagination and being herself that she made seven artworks in no time, including a monster Venus flytrap, a self-portrait cut into cubes, and a bad-mood painting that looked a little like the spilled-can-of-paint-guy's masterpiece with a dollop of Judy Moody thrown in.

Chloe was painting a bowl of cherries sitting on a chair.

"Are you still working on the same painting?" Judy asked.

"It takes a long time to paint a still life," said Chloe.

"Yeah, but you might want to try finishing it while you are *still* in this *life*. It's only

cherries." Judy turned her head sideways. "Or is it goldfish?"

"Thanks a lot," said Chloe.

"You should put some polka dots in the background," said Judy. "And it needs a cat or something."

Chloe said she liked Judy's ideas, but Judy did not see her painting any polka dots. Or cats. Just the same old cherries-not-goldfish bowl.

Judy picked up the squishy foam tray from under Chloe's real-life cherries. "Do you mind if I use this to make a pop-art painting like that Soup Can Guy?"

"Go for it," said Chloe.

A pop-art painting, Judy had just

learned, was a painting of an everyday object, something that you see all the time, like a soup can, and don't even think about. Then when you paint it shocking pink or lemon yellow, all of a sudden it shocks you, and you think about it.

Judy drew a Band-Aid in the foam tray. She poked lots of holes for Band-Aid holes. Then she smeared it with paint and pressed it over and over nine times on one big piece of paper in lots of different neon-bright colors.

"My pop art really pops!" Judy told Chloe.

"You did that?" said Chloe. "It looks fantastic! I mean it."

Chloe still had not painted one single polka dot. Not even a cat hair. "Aren't you done yet?" Judy asked. "You are going to get an *S* for *Slow* or a *T* for *Turtle* in this class."

Chloe laughed. "Okay, let's go. I can finish this later."

Judy gathered up all her paintings. "I'm going to hang them up in my bedroom, like an art show. I think this one's my best." She pointed to her pop-art painting. "I call it *Portrait of a Band-Aid-Not-Soup-Can without Shadows, Deluxe Edition.*"

"I like how you signed it just *Jude*," said Chloe.

"That's my artist name."

"Well, Just Jude, I think you better leave that one here, because it's not dry yet."

"Aw!" said Judy.

"Don't worry, I'll keep an eye on it for you. You can pick it up next time you come for tutoring. I better get you home. I have a twenty-page philosophy paper to write about Plato and Socrates."

Play-Doh and Soccer Teams? "Well, at least you get to write about *fun* stuff," said Judy.

"Yeah, right." As they climbed into Chloe's punch-buggy Gecko Green VW Beetle, Chloe told Judy, "You busted that art class!"

"I owned it," Judy said, beaming from ear to ear.

As far as Judy could tell, there were only three bad things about college: (1) going to school on Saturday, (2) Naked Lady Class, and (3) yakking for a year and a day about shadows.

Other than that, college had hardly any rules, and you got to make a lot of noise about being peaceful. You got to have sleepovers every night with roomies like Bethany Wigmore and play drums with peeps like Paul and hang out in tents that did not have attitude and eat burgers made of veggies all day and change boring, old ordinary stuff into art.

College was uber-*rare*. *Sick-awesome!*

Cat-i-tude

As soon as Judy got home from college, she asked Kate and Richard if she could have a pink mini fridge for her room. They said N-O. Judy called Chloe (for serious) on Kate's not-candy cell phone.

"They actually think a *fridge* belongs *in the kitchen*," she told Chloe. *Old skool.*

The very next day, Judy took a long look around her room. It was *wearing sadface.* Time for a change. She would give her room a makeover—really *college* it up!

First, Judy piled tons of pillows on the floor. Next, she drew zebra stripes all over her bedspread with a marker. Then Judy hung her paintings on the walls and even on the ceiling using Band-Aids for tape. She saved a place of honor over her bunk bed for *Portrait of a Band-Aid-Not-Soup-Can without Shadows, Deluxe Edition.*

Rad! All she needed now was a fuzzy, shaggy, hairy rug like Chloe's. But how to make a boring, old un-fuzzy rug look like a beasty animal with jungle vibes?

She tried dust bunnies from under her bunk bed. She tried lint. She even tried getting Mouse to roll around on her rug to make it nice and cat-hairy.

Judy stood back to admire her new fuzzy

animal rug. It did not look like a tiger. It did not have jungle vibes. It looked like a giant hair ball. And to make matters worse, Kate made Judy vacuum it for *no* allowance.

Judy sat on her bottom bunk to think. Mouse was chasing a ball of yarn. A ball of orange yarn. A ball of fuzzy, hairy yarn. "Mouse, give me that!" said Judy, chasing her around the room on hands and knees, knocking over stacks of pillows and books and a trash can.

"What's going on?" Stink asked. "What are you doing?"

"What's it look like I'm doing?" said Judy.

"Chasing the cat," said Stink. "But why are you chasing the cat?"

"To get the yarn," said Judy.

"But why do you want the yarn?" asked Stink.

"To cut it into a million little pieces."

"But why are you gonna cut it into a million pieces?" Stink asked.

"To make a fuzzy orange rug. What do you think? I'm giving my room a hairy-rug makeover."

"Mo-om!" Stink yelled. "Judy's chasing the cat to get the yarn to cut it into a million pieces to make a fuzzy rug to give her room a hairy-rug makeover!"

What an NCP.

After the hairy-rug makeover experiment, Judy went looking for a peaceful mood. "Peace out!" she called to anybody who was listening. "I'm going out back in the tent!"

The Toad Pee Club tent was like the Attitude Tent without the attitude. Judy climbed inside, where it was secret and quiet, like the peace tents at college. She got down on her hands and knees. Mouse stood still on all fours, watching. Judy arched her back. Mouse arched her back. Judy breathed in and out. Mouse breathed in and out.

Judy gazed at her navel. She tried to fill herself up with peace.

"What in the world . . . ?" said Stink, barging into the tent.

"Stink, you're wrecking my peace."

"I'm wrecking your what?"

"It's yoga," said Judy. "Mouse and I are doing the cat pose."

"Mouse looks like a cat," said Stink, "but you just look like someone staring at her belly button upside down."

"Try it," said Judy. "I learned it at college."

"I can stare at my belly button sitting up," said Stink, "without going to college. Besides, staring at your belly button is about as much fun as watching paint dry."

"They do that at college, too," said Judy.

"Bor-ing," said Stink.

"Hey, what's up?" asked Rocky and Frank, barging into the tent with their big boy-feet.

"Oh, yeah," said Stink. "I came to tell you that Rocky and Frank were coming over."

"Is this an upside-down meeting of the Toad Pee Club?"

"It's yogurt," said Stink. "She learned it at college."

"Yo-ga," said Judy. "Not yogurt. It's like an exercise, not a snack food." Clearly Stink had never read the *Y*-for-*Yoga* encyclopedia.

"Show us," said Frank.

Judy showed them how to arch like a cat. She showed them how to bend in half like a chair, reach to the sky like a warrior, and stand on one leg like a tree. "Now close your eyes, but don't think."

"I can't *not* think," said Frank. "I keep thinking how wacked it is to stand on one leg and pretend to be a tree and try not to think."

"I feel like a flamingo," said Stink. "Or a dorky stork."

"No talking," said Judy. She squeezed her eyes tighter.

CRASH! When Judy opened her eyes, the boys were a jumble of arms and legs on the ground, and they were laughing their pants off.

"Octopus pose!" said Stink, his legs sticking in the air.

"For your 411, there's no such thing as an octopus pose."

Judy closed her eyes again and tried to hear quiet, but all she could hear was more

thrashing and crashing. She opened her eyes again.

Rocky had his neck stretched up to the ceiling. Frank had bendy knees and arms out like a monster. And Stink was all in a twisty ball.

"Giraffe pose," said Rocky.

"Superhero pose," said Frank.

"Human Pretzel pose," said Stink, cracking up.

"P.U.!" said Rocky, waving his hand in front of his face. "You should call that Passing Gas pose." The boys went cuckoo.

"Oh, brother," said Judy. Boys were just plain no good at peace-full yoga.

Flunk-i-tude

When Judy got to Class 3T-now-3G the next morning, there was no teacher in the room. No teacher? No math candy on the desk? No attitude tent? Something was up. Way up!

The whole room was buzzing about what might have happened to Mrs. Grossman. She went camping in her attitude tent? She ate too much good-behavior candy? She ran away to Italy to be a better teacher?

Soon the bell rang. Still no teacher.

"Somebody has to be the teacher," said Jessica Finch, "and I think it should be me, since I'm smartest."

"But Judy Moody's been to college!" yelled Frank.

"And she learned cool stuff," said Rocky, "like how to make yourself into a cat or a chair or a tree."

"Ju-dy Moo-dy! Ju-dy Moo-dy!" The class started yelling and stomping their feet.

She, Professor Judy Moody, stood in front of the whole class and told them all about college. She told about dorm rooms and drums, veggie burgers and vending machines. She told about pancakes and pop art and peace tents. She led the whole class in a tree pose.

"And they learn Floss-O-Fee. It's not about cleaning your teeth. It's about thinking stuff till your head hurts, kind of like a brainteaser but more like a major head-scratcher."

"Like what?" asked Frank.

"Like . . . if a tree falls in the forest, okay, but nobody is around for miles and miles to hear it, does it still make a sound?"

The whole class got quiet. Peace-full quiet. Yoga-not-yogurt quiet. The whole class was lost in a head-scratching attitude of thinking.

Just then, Judy caught a glimpse of

something in the hallway. Something like a shadow. The shadow moved. The shadow was . . .

"MR. TODD!" Judy yelled, breaking the head-scratching silence. "Look, everybody! Professor Todd is back!"

"Mr. Todd! Mr. Todd!"

"Can I try your crutches?"

"Where's Mrs. Grossman?"

"She gave us candy."

"Except Judy, who had to sit in a tent all by herself."

When Class 3T-not-3G had settled down, Mr. Todd told them about his broken foot and going to the doctor's and being late. He showed them his cast, and all the kids got to sign it.

"I'm very proud of you, class, for the way you took over until I got here. And Judy, you'll have to let me in on your secret," said Mr. Todd. "I don't know how you got this class to be so quiet."

"It's college thinking!" said Frank. "Judy Moody goes to college AND third grade now."

They told Mr. Todd everything about Mrs. Grossman and the tutor and going to college. They told him about multistep word problems and math candy and the Attitude Tent.

Mr. Todd smiled and frowned and raised his eyebrows and pushed up his glasses. "I sure missed a lot these last few weeks. Tell you what." Mr. Todd glanced at his watch.

"Looks like we missed Spelling for today. So let's take a short recess, and when we come back, it'll be time for math. I'm going to pass out a quick quiz—"

"Not a test!"

"Don't worry. You won't be graded. I just want to see where everybody is in math."

"Aww," everybody groaned. Everybody except Judy. She wanted to take the quiz. She wanted to show Mr. Todd all the stuff she'd been learning with her tutor— graphs and fractions and algebra. For once, she'd be the one to win gobs and gobs of math candy.

Mr. Todd passed out the tests. Judy got out her college-not-grouchy pencil for good luck. Third-grade pencils were *old skool.* Judy's college pencil flew. She erased only two times. She even drew a graph for extra credit. She did not look at her Ask-a-Question Watch 5000 once.

Judy busted that pop quiz. She owned that math test. Mr. Todd was going to be amazed at Judy's new math-i-tude. Soon she would be the proud owner of buckets of math candy.

Done! Judy looked up. She could not believe her eyes. She, Judy Math-Genius Moody was not done first. She was *dead last.*

"Time's up!" said Mr. Todd. "Let's have fifteen minutes of silent reading while I look over your papers."

For fifteen silent minutes, Judy read ahead in the *Catwings* book. She read with her eyes, but not with her brain. All her brain could think was how super-duper great she was going to be in math.

Mr. Todd was frowning. He looked up. He looked back down. Mr. Todd scratched his head. Mr. Todd frowned some more.

He wrote and wrote with his red pencil.

Judy could not help noticing he hardly even touched his green-for-good-work pencil.

"Class," said Mr. Todd, looking up at last. "We have a problem."

Problem? Of course there was a problem. There were *ten* problems. Everybody knew math was full of problems.

"I've corrected the papers, and the top score goes to Judy Moody."

"Woo-hoo!" said Judy. But she could not see how being top-of-her-class, best-ever in math was a problem.

"The problem is . . . everybody else failed."

What!? The whole, entire class flunked!

As in flubbed it up big-time. As in got a big fat F.

"Most of you did not even finish your tests. And many of you did not even seem to try. Can anybody tell me what's going on here?"

The whole class looked down, staring at their desks, the floor, their shoes. Except for Judy.

"Professor Todd," said Judy, raising her hand. "I know what happened. I got to go to college and become an *uber*-genius in math, and everybody else fell behind."

"Hmm," said Mr. Todd. "Any other ideas? Jessica Finch?"

Jessica cleared her throat. "Well, um,

Rocky and Frank thought it would be way-cool to go to college, and they said—"

"It's our fault," said Rocky. "We thought if we all flunked, we would need a tutor and we would get to go to college, too."

"Like Judy," said Frank.

"You mean you messed up on purpose?" Judy asked.

"Yeah, we just thought it up—during morning recess," said Frank.

"Professor Todd!" said Judy. "I think I should get all the math candy, since I'm the only one who took the test for serious. And they should all go to the Attitude Tent."

"Let's get something straight," said Mr. Todd. "I realize Mrs. Grossman may have had different rules for the last few weeks. But in my class, we do our work to learn, not to earn candy. As for the tent, well, it seems we have an attitude problem bigger than any tent."

Class 3T was silent. Not peace-full quiet. Itchy-scratchy quiet.

"We're sorry," said Frank.

"We'll take it again," said Rocky. "For real this time."

Mr. Todd nodded.

"Professor Todd?" Judy asked. "I have a question. I mean, I was wondering—if you yelled at our class, but nobody was here to hear it, would it still mean you're mad at us?"

Grat-i-tude

"Mom! Dad!" Judy said at supper that night. "I mean Kate! Richard! Guess what! Professor Todd gave us a pop quiz in math today, and I owned it. I only got one wrong, and I did the best of all my peeps and my whole entire class."

"Yeah, but everybody else flunked on purpose," said Stink, "because they all want to go to college, too."

Eesh! Word sure traveled fast around Virginia Dare School.

"Who cares? It was sooooo money!" Judy said.

"She doesn't get money, does she?" asked Stink. "'Cause I'm good in math, so if she gets money, I should get money too!"

"Stink, you're such a *geck*. And don't say, 'What's a geck?' Because that would make you more of a geck." Fact of Life: Stink = Geck. Geck = annoying person!

"Nobody's getting any money," said Dad.

"And nobody's a geck," said Mom.

"Yeah, you're not at college now," Stink said.

"Good news, though," said Mom. "You won't have to go to tutoring anymore."

"Yeah, no more yogurt!" said Stink.

"Huh?" Judy loved college. She liked having a tutor.

"You knew this was just for a short time," Dad said. "To get extra help for a few weeks. But now Mr. Todd's back, and we're proud of how great you're doing."

"You'll still see Chloe, honey," Mom said. "Maybe she'll come to your class to help Mr. Todd. And she said she'd be happy to babysit anytime."

"Does she know Stink lives here, too?"

"And that's not even the best news," said Mom. "When Chloe called today—"

"Chloe called? You talked to Chloe? When? Where was I?"

"You were at school—" said Mom.

"No fair." Judy couldn't help it that her cell phone was made of candy.

"Let Mom finish," said Dad.

"Anyway, remember a painting you made when you went to college for a day with Chloe?"

"Yes! *Portrait of a Band-Aid-Not-Soup-Can without Shadows, Deluxe Edition.*"

"What's that?" Stink asked.

"It's a pop-art painting like that guy who paints soup cans, Andy Warthog."

Stink snorted like a warthog.

"Warhol," said Dad. "Andy Warhol."

"Is anybody going to let me finish?" Mom asked.

"Peace!" said Judy, holding up two fingers.

"As I was saying, I guess you left it there to dry, and the professor thought the painting was made by one of his college students. He chose your painting to hang in an art show at the college. They have a small gallery in the college library there."

She, Judy Moody, could not believe her ears. "Painting? College? Art show? Me?" she asked.

Dad laughed. "We thought you'd be pleased."

Pleased? Pleased was only a teeny-tiny fraction of what she felt. This was *uber*-exciting. This was ridonkulus-rare. She,

Judy Moody Warthog, aka Just Jude, was going to be in an art show *at college*! For serious!

"I have to call Chloe," Judy said.

"On your candy cell phone?" Stink asked.

"Stink. I take it back. You're not just a geck. You're a geck squared. Geck to the power of three."

"Gecko-gecko, click-click, cheep-cheep-cheep," sang Stink, bobbing his head and making gecko noises all around the kitchen.

What a warthog.

☻   ☻   ☻

The next morning at school, Judy flip-flopped down the hall to Room 3T.

"Professor Todd," Judy asked, "did you tell Kate and Richard that I don't need a tutor anymore? Because I really learned a lot in college, and I'd like to keep going. And besides, my painting is in an art show there, and I'd really like to see—"

"You know, Judy, you're not the only one who wants to go to college," said Mr. Todd.

"What do you mean? Didn't you already go to college, like a long time ago, I mean, to be a teacher and everything?"

"Not me—the class. Class 3T is going to college."

"You mean the whole class needs a

tutor? But I thought everybody just flunked the test on purpose."

"Not for tutoring," said Mr. Todd. "We're going on a field trip."

"To college?"

"To college," said Mr. Todd.

"And Chloe will be there?"

"Chloe will be there. We'll be spending a whole morning in the Math Lab."

"And we can go see my painting?"

"We can go see your painting. Won't that be exciting?"

"You don't know the half of it! The three-quarters of it. The nine-tenths of it. Thank you, Mr. Todd, thank you!"

She, Judy Moody, had a brand new attitude. It was *grat*-i-tude.

Glad-i-tude

One whole week had to go by before Judy Moody got to go to college with her class. The week took about a year. At last it was time.

When Class 3T got to college, their first stop was the Math Lab. Judy took everyone over to Investigation Station and showed them how to build with sponge blocks and make graphs and play Tic-Tac-Cookie. They even got a taste of Chloe's special pizza fractions (minus the pizza tables, which Judy got to collect).

Then Chloe passed out poster boards. Everyone got to spread out all over the floor and make their very own board games. Judy Moody drew different tents on her game board and a twisty-turny path that connected them.

Chloe peeked over her shoulder. "What are these?" she asked.

"See, you start out in the Attitude Tent," said Judy. "The object of the game is to try not to land in the Bad-i-tude Tent. To win, you have to get all the way to the Glad-i-tude Tent."

Next she made a spinner. Then she made up Attitude Cards.

"See, bad stuff can happen to you along the way," said Judy. "But it all depends on your attitude. If you pick a bad Attitude Card, you have to go to the Bad-i-tude Tent. If you pick a good Attitude Card, you get to skip way ahead. Three good Attitude Cards, and you win the Peace Prize."

"Rad!" said Chloe.

"See?" said Judy. "In the Judy Moody game of life, it's all about attitude."

❧   ❧   ❧

"Time for lunch!" Chloe called. Chloe and Mr. Todd carried big boxes over to the picnic tables by the duck pond. Class 3T counted twelve shiny green-headed ducks, twenty-seven Canada geese, three regular honkers, and eleven turtles.

"We could make a graph!" said Judy.

"Let's eat first," said Mr. Todd. Chloe passed out box lunches. Inside each box was . . . a veggie burger. Soon, Class 3T was yoga-quiet as they vegged out on veggie burgers and juice-box smoothies. And the ducks vegged out on all the bread crumbs they dropped.

"Yum! Bet you didn't know that health food actually tastes good," said Judy.

"And for dessert," said Chloe, "everybody gets a cup of Screamin' Mimi's Rain Forest Mist ice cream."

"Blue ice cream!"

"YAY!"

"It's my favorite!"

"Is it made of vegetables, too?"

When everybody was done licking the last drops of ice cream, Frank asked Chloe, "Do you have recess at college?"

"Sure," said Chloe. "At college, you can make your own recess, anytime you want. Just about."

"Whoa," said Judy and Rocky and Frank.

Across the field, Judy saw two college kids walking toward them. They were carrying Frisbees and Hula-Hoops and . . . drums!

"Hey," said Judy, pointing, "it's Bethany Wigmore and Paul the drummer guy."

Class 3T had the best recess ever—recess squared, college style. When they were done Hula-Hooping and drumming and chasing after Frisbees, it was time to go see the art show.

Judy Moody and Class 3T walked across the Quad, around Coffee Catz, and past the art building to the library. Quietly, they filed up the stairs to the second-floor art gallery.

Mom was there, and Dad, and Stink with a camera!

"What are you guys doing here?" Judy whispered.

"We didn't want to miss your big show," said Dad.

"And I got out of learning about commas!" said Stink.

Judy stepped inside the quiet room, where paintings lined the white walls.

There were still lifes of fruit and landscapes of trees. There were paintings of blobs and cut-paper collages of cats.

Then she saw it. *Portrait of a Band-Aid-Not-Soup-Can without Shadows, Deluxe Edition.*

"Guess which one's mine," said Judy.

"The Band-Aids!" Stink shouted, running up to the painting.

"It certainly is colorful," said Dad.

"Creative," said Mom.

"Very college," said Mr. Todd, winking.

"Look!" said Stink. "You got a ribbon."

"Me? Best in Show?" Judy asked.

Stink peered closer at the ribbon. "Never mind," he said, blocking it with his big head so Judy couldn't see.

"What?" Judy asked. "Let me see."

"You don't want to see," said Stink. "It says you got HORRIBLE MENTION. That really stinks."

"Horrible Mention?" She, Judy Moody, won the prize for the most horrible painting in the art show? "Why even *mention* it if it's *horrible*?" Judy wailed.

Mr. Todd laughed. So did Mom and Dad. So did Chloe.

"Why is everybody laughing?" Judy asked. "Horrible Mention means they think my painting is horrible."

"It's an *Honorable* Mention," Chloe explained.

Honorable Mention sounded way better than Horrible Mention. "That's good, right?" Judy said. Stink moved over so Judy could see.

"Wicked good," said Chloe. "It means your painting was so rad, they thought they should *honor* it with a big fat ribbon."

Sick-awesome!

"Let's stand next to your painting so we can get a picture," said Mom. Everybody crowded around Judy, and the library lady snapped a picture on Stink's camera.

"Let me see!" said Judy.

She peered at the image in the camera. Next to her and all around her were Kate and Richard and Stink; Rocky, Frank, Jessica Finch, and the rest of Class 3T; Professor Todd and Chloe; even peeps Bethany Wigmore and Paul the Drummer.

In the very center, right in front of her Not-Horrible-Mention painting, stood Judy herself, smiling from ear to ear.

If that picture were a painting, she, Judy Moody, would give it a name. *Portrait of the Artist with the 'Rents, the Professor, the College Tutor, a Few Peeps, and the Geck, with Shadows, Deluxe Edition.*

It was only a split-second, one-sixtieth-of-a-minute, a giga-flip-flop moment in Judy Moody's own personal game of life, but it felt big. She, Judy Moody, was filled with *glad*-i-tude.

Rad-i-tude!

Judy Moody's Not-Webster's New World College Dictionary

FIRST EDITION

the bomb: the best

busted: did well; *owned*

crucial: *Rare!* Excellent! Awesome!

for serious: for real

for your 411: for your information

geck: annoying person; Stink

hit me up later: call me later; see you later

let's food: let's eat

mad-nasty: see *sick-awesome*

natch: of course; naturally

NCP: nincompoop; a silly or foolish person

OLD SKOOL

GECK!

Natch!

So Money

old skool: old-fashioned; out-of-date

owned: ruled

paper (verb): write a report

peace out: good-bye; I'm leaving

peeps: friends

rad: radical; *crucial*

'rents; 'rentals: parents

ridonkulus: ridiculous

roomie: roommate

sick-awesome: more impressive than *sick;*
more powerful than *rare*

so money: excellent

uber: way cool; over-the-top awesome

wearing sadface: sadly lacking; looking unhappy

wicked good: better than good

Megan McDonald is the author of the popular Judy Moody and Stink series, as well as the Judy Moody and Friends series for new readers. She has written many other books for children, including the Ant and Honey Bee stories, the Sisters Club series, and several picture books. Before she began writing full-time, Megan McDonald worked as a librarian, a bookseller, and a living-history actress. She lives in Northern California with her husband, Richard Haynes, who is also a writer.

Peter H. Reynolds is the illustrator of the popular Judy Moody and Stink series in addition to many other books, including several for which he is also author. They include his Creatrilogy of picture books: *The Dot, Ish,* and *Sky Color.* His book *The Dot* has even inspired International Dot Day, which is celebrated around the world every September. Besides writing and illustrating, Peter H. Reynolds is a bookstore owner, animator, and educator. He lives in Massachusetts with his family.

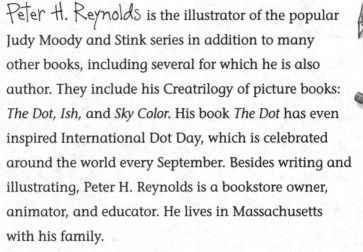